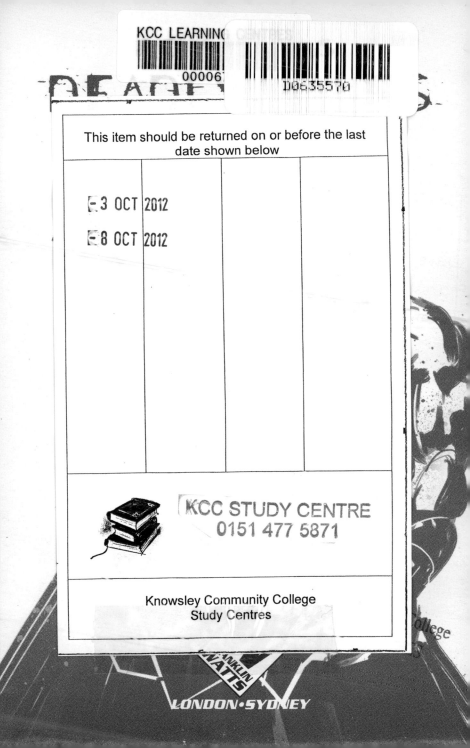

FRANKLIN
WATTS

LONDON·SYDNEY

To everyone at Basildon Lower Academy, and with thanks to all the members of the Year 8 Writers' Project for their help with creating this series. R. A.

First published in 2012
by Franklin Watts

Text © Roy Apps 2012
Illustrations by Ollie Cuthbertson © Franklin Watts 2012
Cover design by Jonathan Hair
and Peter Scoulding

Franklin Watts
338 Euston Road
London NW1 3BH

Franklin Watts Australia
Level 17/207 Kent Street
Sydney, NSW 2000

A CIP catalogue record for this book
is available from the British Library.

ISBN: 978 1 4451 0341 9

1 3 5 7 9 10 8 6 4 2

Printed in Great Britain

Franklin Watts is a division of Hachette Children's Books,
an Hachette UK company.
www.hachette.co.uk

CONTENTS

Raijin

Chapter 1 – A date with Sumi   5

Chapter 2 – Ueno Park   7

Chapter 3 – Thunderstorm   11

Chapter 4 – Deep, jagged tears   20

Woman in the Mirror

Chapter 1 – Halloween   25

Chapter 2 – The story of Mary Worth   30

Chapter 3 – "Mirror, mirror…"   36

Raijin

✝

=1=

A date with Sumi

Koji lay on his bed, stared at the ceiling and grinned. He'd got himself a date. And what a date it was! He was going out with Sumi, the prettiest, liveliest girl in his year. All the boys wanted a date with Sumi. She'd spent a year living in California, and was much less boring than the other girls at the Tokyo high school where Koji was studying.

Koji was quiet and serious, and worked hard at his studies. He'd never asked a girl for a date before; he thought that they would laugh at him. He wished he could tell the rest of the boys in his year that he, Koji, was going out with Sumi, but of course, he couldn't.

He knew what they would say:

"You, Koji? Going out with Sumi? You're making it up. It's another one of your little fantasies. Why would Sumi ever want to go out with a geek like you?"

Still, what did they matter? This evening he would be meeting Sumi at Ueno Park in downtown Tokyo for his very first date.

2

Ueno Park

Koji left his parents' apartment and made his way to the busy, bustling streets of central Tokyo. He glanced in the shop windows, saw his reflection and thought happily of the evening ahead. Above him, storm clouds scudded across the early evening sky. But Koji didn't see them. He was standing at the main park gates next to the National Tokyo Museum, scanning the pavement to the left and right, waiting for his first sight of Sumi. He had a moment's panic. Perhaps he had got it all wrong? Perhaps Sumi never had any intention of going out with him? No, he told himself, that couldn't be right.

And then he saw her, long dark hair bouncing about her shoulders. She waved, and Koji waved back.

They had a couple of Cokes in the busy café. Koji wondered what they would do next until Sumi said, "Let's walk."

So they strolled through Ueno Park, along the pathway bordered on both sides by ancient cherry trees, all the way down past the Kiyomizu Kannon-do Temple. Sumi talked about her time in California and asked Koji all sorts of questions about himself. Koji told Sumi things he'd never spoken to anyone else about: his strict parents, his elderly grandmother who lived up by the lakes in the North, his plans for going to college, his determination to one day visit the US. By the time they reached Shinobazu Pond, dusk had begun to fall.

"Let's go round the other side," Sumi said, "it'll be much quieter there." She grabbed Koji's hand.

Shinobazu Pond is more of a lake than a pond, and by the time Koji and Sumi reached the far side, they were alone. The only sound they could hear was the gentle splashing of the ducks in the water.

Thunderstorm

A short, sharp clap of thunder shook the air.

"Wow! We're in for a thunderstorm!" declared Sumi, excitedly.

Koji couldn't see what there was to get excited about. "We'll get wet," he said.

As if to prove his point, large drops of rain began to fall on them.

"Let's go for a dip!" Sumi said.

"We haven't got our swimming things!" protested Koji.

"Who needs swimming things?" said Sumi, with a shrug. "We can go skinny-dipping."

A sudden flash of lightning lit up her sparkling eyes. "We went skinny-dipping all the time in California."

"But—" Koji began.

"Come on, Koji! It'll be fun! Skinny-dipping in the rain!"

"But it's not just rain, is it? It's a storm!"

"So?" Sumi's lips broadened into a teasing smile.

"You know what we were taught by our parents, what every Japanese person is taught by their parents," Koji pleaded anxiously.

"Oh, Koji, for goodness' sake! You're not worried about Raijin, are you?"

Every Japanese boy and girl knows about Raijin.

Koji said nothing. He was acutely aware that they were both getting totally drenched in the teeming rain.

"The Raijin story is just a silly, old-fashioned myth that grown-ups tell to scare kids," said Sumi. "You surely can't believe all that nonsense? You're bright, you're going to go to college. You're planning to go to the United States one day."

Koji looked down, glumly. The rain dripped from his eyelids like oversized tears. "How do we know it's not true?" he whispered. His grandmother had told him the story of Raijin, the thunder god who wreaks revenge on humans. He tears out their navels then makes them disappear, should they dare to taunt him with a sight of their naked stomachs during a thunderstorm. And Koji had seen the power that storms could wreak on the rivers, forests and homes of the region where his grandmother lived. He was in no doubt that there were forces in this world too great for simple humans to understand.

Of course, there was something else troubling Koji, too. Supposing he went skinny-dipping and Sumi laughed at his body?

As if reading his mind, Sumi said with a laugh: "You're not shy, are you?" And she pulled off her T-shirt, slipped out of her jeans and skipped down to the water's edge. A flash of lightning lit up her skin.

He wanted to run after her. But something held him back. "No, Sumi! No!" he shouted. "Wait until the storm is over. We can go skinny-dipping then!"

Koji's words were lost in a huge roar of thunder, which echoed all the way round the lake. It sounded like an evil laugh. A dazzling flash of lightning lit up the sky and Koji saw Sumi in the lake, her hand raised as if beckoning him to join her for a swim.

Another flash of lightning and Koji saw now that Sumi wasn't waving. She was reaching out to him for help. She was screaming in desperation, clawing at the air. There was something out there, and it was dragging her deeper into the lake. A growl of thunder rippled through the air.

Sumi let out another agonised scream before her head disappeared under the water. Koji stumbled into the lake, shouting, "Sumi! Sumi!" He thought for a moment that he'd managed to grab hold of her, but then she was tugged out of his hands by something much stronger than him. He searched for her through tear-streaked eyes, but the sky was dark with rain.

4

Deep, jagged tears

At dusk, the park security guards found
Koji sitting at the edge of Shinobazu Pond,
perfectly still. He was staring out to the
middle of the water, as if he expected Sumi
to come back. Her clothes were still piled up
next to him.

The police found her body the following
day. On her bare stomach, where her navel
should have been, were deep, jagged cuts.
They looked as if they'd been made in
a frenzy by someone or something with
powerful clawed fingernails.

The police didn't believe Koji when he
told them it was the curse of Raijin. Why
should they? It was just a myth, after all.

Neither did they believe him when he told them that he had tried to save Sumi; that they had been out on a date. Why should they? After all, the students and teachers they interviewed at his high school all shook their heads and said: "Koji? Going out with Sumi? Never!"

Each day and night, Koji goes through what happened in Ueno Park. There is little else he can do, as he sits alone in his windowless cell, awaiting trial for Sumi's murder.

THE END...

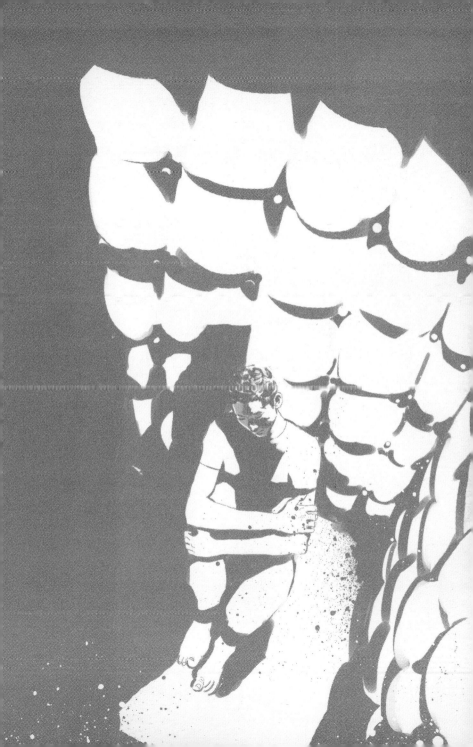

Woman in the Mirror

✝

Halloween

"This has to be the most boring Halloween party ever!" groaned Jaclyn Stone.

Marlee and I could only agree. We were all with our families at Jaclyn's house. Marlee and I had been best friends for ages, ever since we met in First Grade. Jaclyn had only just moved into our town. She was tall and very beautiful. It was like she had the body of someone two or three years older than us. For some reason, she'd latched onto Marlee and me. She seemed to enjoy sneering at Marlee, but Marlee put up with it. I don't know why.

Jaclyn's folks were holding a Halloween

house-warming party. The adults had all trooped into Mr Stone's home movie theatre to watch *Dawn of the Dead*.

"Why don't you girls go over to the den to make sure the little ones are OK?" suggested Jaclyn's mom. It was obvious she didn't think we were old enough to watch *Dawn of the Dead* with them.

"Hey, there's no way I'm going to spend Halloween being an unpaid babysitter," said Jaclyn, moodily.

So we ended up sitting in the kitchen, drinking mocktails and eating pretzels. The most boring Halloween party ever. But then things got worse. The door flew open and in burst Ellie May, Marlee's kid sister.

"Will you play witches with us? Please!" whined Ellie May.

That's how the three of us ended up two blocks away at Marlee's house. As soon as we

went in, Jaclyn turned up her nose like she'd gotten a bad smell under it.

"You live here?" she said, as if Marlee's house was some sort of cow shed. True, it wasn't much of a house; Marlee's dad had left home and her mom worked part-time in the high school kitchen: there wasn't a lot of money.

Marlee looked hurt. Jaclyn, of course, took no notice, but I knew how sore Marlee felt.

Jaclyn told the first scary story. It was all about a beautiful girl who was killed by a hit-and-run driver when she was hitchhiking. She came back every year as a ghost. Next, I told the story of a couple who were necking in the back of taxi and were attacked by a madman with a hook for a hand.

And then it was Marlee's turn.

"Do you know the story of Mary Worth?" she asked, quietly.

I looked up at Marlee in alarm, but Jaclyn said, dismissively: "Never heard of it. Is it scary?"

"Sure, it's scary," Marlee said. "It's about something that really happened in this town, way back in the nineteen sixties."

"Well, it had better be good," replied Jaclyn, with a pout.

I shivered. Marlee was my oldest friend; sure, Jaclyn bullied her and needed to be taught a lesson; sure she deserved to have that oh-so-superior smile wiped off her perfect face, but Mary Worth? I couldn't decide which was the more chilling thought: the idea that Marlee didn't know what she was doing, or the idea that she did.

The story of Mary Worth

"This is the story of Mary Worth," Marlee began. Jaclyn stifled a small yawn. I said nothing.

"Mary Worth was beautiful and rich, and she knew it." Jaclyn smiled. Yes, she could see herself as Mary, quite easily. Marlee went on: "Mary was High School Prom Queen. After the prom, she saw her best friend in a clinch with the football captain. She waited for her friend to go to the washroom, then she snuck up to the football captain, Jon Hoffman, flashed her eyes at him and asked him to drive her home."

"Hey, good for her," murmured Jaclyn.

"Mary suggested they take in a drive-in movie on the way home. Wanting to make sure she looked her best for what was to come, she checked her face in the vanity mirror. It wasn't big enough, not for Mary Worth. So she turned the driver's rear-view mirror round so that she could see the whole of her lovely face. Now she could add the necessary touches with her lipstick and eyeshadow. Unfortunately, without a rear-view mirror, Jon failed to spot the truck that was approaching fast on their tail. As he made a left turn, the truck hit the car broadsides. Mary Worth's face was cut into a maze of bloody ribbons by shards of broken windshield glass."

"Sounds kinda nasty," commented Jaclyn.

"Her folks were terrified how she would react if she caught sight of her once beautiful face. So they took away every mirror in the house, except for a full-length one in the

back bedroom, which Mary's mother used. But Mary was desperate to see her face again. So, late one night, after everyone had gone to bed, she crept into that back bedroom."

"As soon as she saw her face, she let out a terrible scream. Then she stepped straight into the mirror, desperate for it to give her back the beautiful reflection she'd once had. And, even today, any three people in this town who gather with a lighted candle in front of a mirror, can by uttering the incantation 'I believe in Mary Worth' thirteen times, summon the spirit of Mary Worth. Only she doesn't appear as a beautiful girl, but as a haggard and scar-faced old woman. And, she singles out one of the three people who have summoned her and scars them for life."

Jaclyn looked at Marlee and snorted. "You say that happened here in your town? I've heard different versions of it in other places.

It's just a story."

"Well," Marlee said, steadily, "if it's just a story, what are we waiting for? There are three of us here, there's a candle in that pumpkin head over there and there's a full-length mirror in my mom's bedroom."

Jaclyn leapt up with a whoop. "OK, let's do it!" And with that, she took the candle from the pumpkin and the box of matches that was lying beside it, and ran out of the kitchen towards the stairs.

"Mirror, mirror..."

As Marlee got up to follow Jaclyn, I grabbed her arm. "Marlee," I whispered, urgently, "I know Jaclyn needs teaching a lesson, but this is wrong. This is dangerous."

"Aw, come on, Beth," Marlee said. "You heard what Jaclyn said." She mimicked Jaclyn's nasal sneer: "It's only a story! And Jaclyn must be right; she's so, so clever."

"Come on, you two," yelled Jaclyn. "Or are you both too scared?"

Marlee grabbed my hand and practically pulled me up the stairs. There was a steely look in her eyes that I'd never seen before. When we got to the bedroom, Jaclyn had already lit the candle.

"Shut the door, Beth," said Jaclyn.

I shut the door.

Jaclyn turned out the light. We all sat down and faced the mirror.

"I believe in Mary Worth," began Jaclyn.

"Oh, come on, you two! We've all got to chant, isn't that what you said, Marlee?"

"I don't think we should be doing this," I whispered.

"Beth, you are such a wuzza!" snapped Jaclyn.

"I just don't want anything bad to happen!" I protested.

"I can't think of anything worse happening than having to be in a dump like this," retorted Jaclyn, casting her eyes round Marlee's mom's sparsely-furnished bedroom. I tried to catch Marlee's eye, but she was staring intently into the mirror.

"I believe in Mary Worth…" she said, slowly, steadily.

And because Marlee was my friend, I joined in.

"I believe in Mary Worth…" Louder, more shrill. All three of us together now.

Four times, five times, six. The candle spluttered as we chanted.

"I believe in Mary Worth…" Eleven.

"I believe in Mary Worth…" Twelve.

"I believe in Mary Worth…" Thirteen.

I waited for Jaclyn to laugh. But she didn't. Instead, the mirror cracked and splintered from top to bottom. For a brief moment, I saw the shape of an old woman, her face haggard and scar-crossed. Her crabby hand clutched a large, shining blade of glass. It slashed out at Jaclyn's beautiful face and she howled. She tried to move, but we were all rooted to the spot by some dark force. So she fought back, but the glass blade cut into her hands. Jaclyn wailed and I screamed for Mary to stop. I covered my ears. Then the old woman was gone.

In the flickering candlelight, I saw Jaclyn's bloodstained hands clutch at her face. She screamed as bright red blood seeped out from between her fingers. When she pulled her hands away, her cheeks and mouth were crisscrossed by a mass of deep, red, ugly lines. Blood ran into her mouth and dripped from her chin.

Next to her, seemingly impassive to this sight and to Jaclyn's hideous screams, sat Marlee. A sly, satisfied smile had settled on her far from innocent face.

THE END...

DEADLY TALES

One book.
Two nightmares.

978 1 4451 0340 2 pb
978 1 4451 0855 1 eBook

978 1 4451 0337 2 pb
978 1 4451 0852 0 eBook

978 1 4451 0336 5 pb
978 1 4451 0851 3 eBook

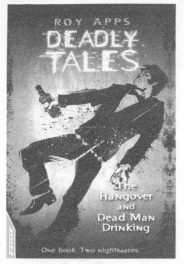

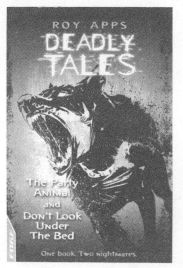

978 1 4451 0339 6 pb
978 1 4451 0854 4 eBook

978 1 4451 0338 9 pb
978 1 4451 0853 7 eBook

Find out more about these books and
others published by EDGE at:
www.franklinwatts.co.uk

Plus visit Roy's website for the latest
news on all his books:
www.royapps.co.uk

DEADLY TALES
TEASER

Can't wait to find out what happens in the other DEADLY TALES urban legends? Well, here's a teaser from Love Bites:

"It looks slightly better today. I'm sure it'll be gone soon," said her mother one morning, before leaving for work.

You're a liar, Isabella thought. The blotch didn't look any better and the itching had got worse. It had kept her awake half the night. She went to the bathroom and looked at herself in the mirror as she always did. A couple of months ago she would have admired her deep hazel eyes in her perfectly formed face. Now all she could see was a

red blotch, the size of a volcano. A red blotch
that itched and throbbed and pulsated.

Isabella put the long, polish-chipped
nails of her right hand up to her cheek.
She couldn't stand the deep, incessant
itching any longer.

✝

Dare you to read the rest in:
DEADLY TALES
Love Bites
and
It Crawled From the Dark

Want to read more horror? Try iHorror by
The 2Steves, where you are the hero and
have to choose your own fate.

Fight your fear. Choose your fate.

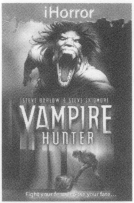

978 1 40830 985 8 pb
978 1 40831 476 0 eBook

978 1 40830 986 5 pb
978 1 40831 477 7 eBook

978 1 40830 988 9 pb
978 1 40831 479 1 eBook

978 1 40830 987 2 pb
978 1 40831 478 4 eBook

www.orchardbooks.co.uk